THE HORRIBLE CAT

Spider

THE HORRIBLE CAT

by Nanette Newman
illustrated by Michael Foreman

PAVILION

First published in Great Britain in 1992 by
PAVILION BOOKS LIMITED
196 Shaftesbury Avenue, London WC2H 8JL

Text copyright © Bryan Forbes Ltd, 1992
Illustrations copyright © Michael Foreman 1992

The moral right of the author has been asserted.

Designed by Janet James

A CIP catalogue record for this book
is available from the British Library.

ISBN 1 85145 814 X

Printed and bound in Belgium by Proost

2 4 6 8 10 9 7 5 3 1

This book may be ordered by post
direct from the publisher. Please contact
the Marketing Department.
But try your bookshop first.

ONCE UPON A TIME, NOT SO LONG AGO —
well, last winter, in fact — there lived a cat
named Spider.

He wasn't the sort of cat you usually
read about. He was untidy, wriggly, fat
in some places, thin in others, snarly,
scratchy, and very, very mean.

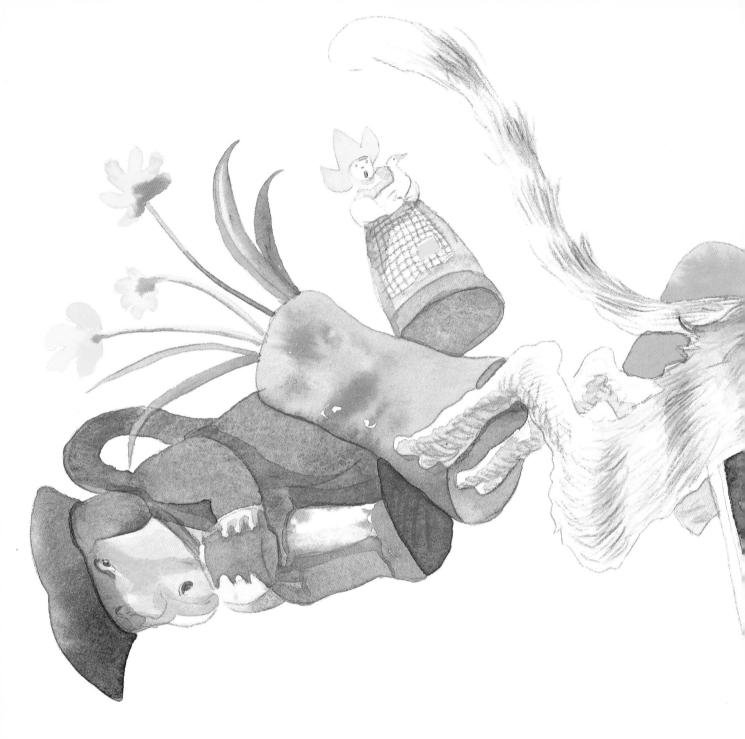

He could be nasty about almost anything. For instance, if his breakfast wasn't there at eight on the dot, he would screech wildly and run up and down the stairs twenty times. He would thump his tail against the fridge, claw the best cushion in the big chair, and leap onto the mantelpiece, knocking over the photograph of himself with his owner, a dear, sweet, old lady named Mrs. Broom.

Now, Mrs. Broom, unlike her cat, was kind and gentle and very, very quiet. She was fat in some places and thin in others, but apart from that she was nothing like her cat at all.

You might wonder how such a horrible cat came to live with such a lovely person. In fact, most people wondered just that—most people except Mrs. Broom, who wasn't the wondering type.

The truth of the matter was he just arrived.

It was on a day when everyone woke up, looked out of their windows, and said, "What a beastly, cold, rainy, dreary day," that Mrs. Broom went to her front door to bring in the milk and . . . discovered a cat.

"Well, would you believe it," she said. "A dear little cat."

Now, this was a *big* mistake, for he wasn't a dear little cat at all. He sat there in the rain, making faces and crossing his eyes, a habit he had when he was very, very annoyed (which, of course, he always was).

As soon as he saw Mrs. Broom, he had one of his tantrums. He lay on his back, waved his paws in the air, and screamed in a very alarming way.

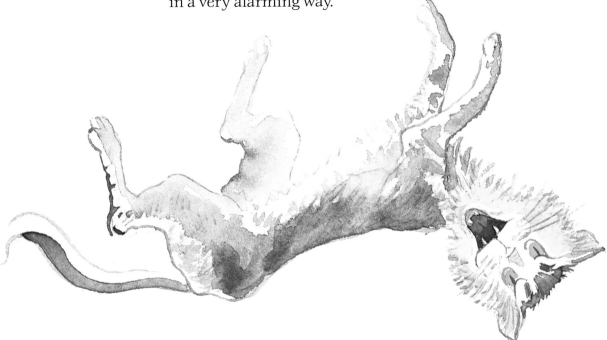

But Mrs. Broom didn't seem to notice. She just picked up the bottles and disappeared into the kitchen. After a while, the cat decided to stop showing off and followed her. What he saw would have made most cats happy, but not this cat. Mrs. Broom was singing as she chopped up fish and poured some cream into a bowl.

The horrible cat banged his tail on the floor and snarled, showing all his teeth. Mrs. Broom turned to look at him, and because she couldn't see very well without her glasses, which she had left by the bed, she said, "Oh, you dear little thing, you're smiling at me."

Mrs. Broom put down the delicious breakfast. At first the cat pretended he couldn't care less and turned his back on it. Then, when Mrs. Broom wasn't looking, he pounced on the food, spilling as much as possible, slopping cream onto the floor, and letting bits of fish fall out of the sides of his mouth. It was a very unattractive sight. Most people would have tried not to look, but Mrs. Broom just cleaned up the mess and said, "Well, you really enjoyed that, didn't you?"

The cat gave her one of his meanest looks.

"I think you'd better stay with me," Mrs. Broom said. And that's how it happened — as simple as that.

After that first morning things went from bad to worse. For instance, the horrible cat had never had a name and Mrs. Broom had never had a cat, so she wasn't very good at thinking of catlike names. She had, however, always been rather fond of spiders. "I'll call you Spider," she said, as he tried to claw the quilt off her bed. "You'll like that!" He didn't, of course — because he didn't like anything.

Spider's days were always busy. He chased every dog that came near the house. He walked all over Mrs. Broom's ironing with muddy paws. He ran up trees and made

such a fuss that all the birds left their nests. One day Mr. Knight, who lived nearby, saw Spider hanging from a top branch, and, being a kind man, he got a ladder to help him down. But when Mr. Knight reached him, Spider stuck out his tongue and slid down on his own. Next he jumped into Mrs. Broom's bath, licked the soap, and covered the towels with hair. He frightened the baby who lived next door by taking her teddy bear and sitting on it. And all that was before lunch!

Every day, he tore the newspaper into small pieces and chewed up the bills. When he saw the white cat from across the street he spat three times, stuck out his claws, and made his fur stand up like a brush.

In the evening Mrs. Broom liked to watch television. She particularly liked quiz shows, but Spider soon learned to change the channels with his nose. Mrs. Broom never seemed to notice.

When Mrs. Broom went to bed, Spider would climb on top of the wardrobe and then leap onto her quilt. He'd toss and turn and jump around until finally even he was exhausted. Then he'd poke his head out from under the covers to see if Mrs. Broom was annoyed. But she was always fast asleep with a smile on her face.

Mrs. Broom's friend Emily came to tea one day. She was horrified when Spider jumped on her head and rearranged her hair in a most unattractive way, then knocked over the milk jug and kicked the biscuits in the air with his back paws. Mrs. Broom laughed. "He's doing all his little tricks for you," she said. "Isn't he funny?" Emily didn't think he was at all funny and said to Mr. Knight later that she'd seen some horrible animals in her time, but never one as horrible as Spider. Mr. Knight, who never had a bad word to say about anyone, had a *very* bad word to say about Spider — so bad, in fact, that Emily wondered whether she had heard him correctly.

Spider was still living with Mrs. Broom when the summer came. Mrs. Broom loved being in her garden. She grew lots of flowers, herbs, and lettuces — or she did before she had Spider. He decided the best place for a nap was the lettuce bed, so that was the end of those.

Most afternoons, Spider lay by the side
of the fish pond with one paw dangling
in the water so that the fish were always in a panic, fearing for their lives.
Mrs. Broom didn't notice. She just blew
him a kiss as she picked some roses
for the house.

It was a day in July, when everyone looked out of their windows and said, "Oh, what a beautiful, hot summer day," when something happened that changed Spider's life.

He'd been sitting on the wall trying to outstare the thrush in the apple tree when he heard a gentle thud. He looked around and there, lying half on the herb bed and half on the path, was Mrs. Broom. Spider leapt from the wall straight onto Mrs. Broom's tummy, but she didn't move. He made some of his scary faces and did a bit of yowling, but Mrs. Broom was very still and her eyes were tightly shut.

For the first time in Spider's life he was frightened. He felt very strange as he looked at Mrs. Broom's white face. He tried licking her cheek, but even though it was a hot day she felt cold. He thumped his tail and rolled on his back like he did when he wanted some food, but Mrs. Broom just lay very still.

Spider knew that something was dreadfully wrong and he must get help. But how? He ran around Mrs. Broom's body trying to think, and then he sped off to Emily's house as fast as he could.

Emily was knitting in a deck chair in her garden. Spider jumped onto her lap and started to meow. Emily pushed him off, shouting, "Get away you nasty, naughty cat. Get away!"

So Spider ran off to Mr. Knight's house. Mr. Knight was tying up his string beans. When he saw Spider he picked up his shovel and said, "Come anywhere near these and you'll know what for." Desperate, Spider picked up the ball of string in his mouth and started to run, unwinding it as he went. Mr. Knight shouted, "Drop that string! Come back here!" and started to run after him.

Spider ran and ran, out of the garden, across the road, through Emily's garden, round the big chestnut tree, and into Mrs. Broom's garden. He came to a stop by Mrs. Broom's left foot. He heard Mr. Knight come clumping up the path with the other end of the string in his hand, saying, "I'll   get you for this!"

But he stopped when he saw Mrs. Broom with Spider waiting beside her. Mr. Knight immediately called an ambulance, and soon Mrs. Broom was on her way to the hospital.

Suddenly alone, Spider didn't know what to do with himself. The house felt very empty. There was no one to make him nice meals, no one to tell him he was adorable, and no one to annoy. As the days went by he grew so depressed that he didn't even feel like frightening the white cat across the road. One day a big dog came into the garden and started to bark, but Spider did nothing. There were no singing sounds in the house, and the flowers in the vase all dropped their petals. Life just wasn't the same.

At night Spider had to forage around in dustbins for food that had been thrown away, and during the day he didn't feel like rushing around and being nasty and annoying. After all, there was no one to be nasty to. He grew thinner and thinner and sat around in an unhappy heap, thinking about things.

It was a Thursday, when the leaves were
beginning to turn brown and when people were opening their windows and
saying, "Well, isn't this a fine autumn
morning," when Spider heard the front
door open. He looked up from where he
was lying on the kitchen floor and there,
to his amazement, was Mrs. Broom. She
looked much the same as ever, and when
she saw Spider she smiled and smiled.

"Oh, my goodness me," she said. "Just look at you. I've been so worried about
you, I couldn't wait to get back. You look like you could use a good meal." Before
Spider could move she had taken off her coat and was bustling around in the
kitchen, fixing him something tasty. The old Spider would have done a bit of
snarling and knocked the plate over and spat and thumped his tail, but to tell
the truth, he was so thrilled to see Mrs. Broom and to have a good meal that he
forgot to do any of these things.

That evening, when Mrs. Broom had tidied the house and was watching television with her feet up, Spider did something he had never done in his life before. He crawled into her lap, curled up into a ball, and started to purr. "Well, well," said Mrs. Broom. "What's all this?" And she stroked the back of his head until they both fell asleep.

Of course, word got around how clever Spider had been when Mrs. Broom had her fall, and how he had found a way to get Mr. Knight to follow him. In fact, Spider became quite famous. Even Emily was impressed that a cat, particularly a cat as horrible as Spider, could have thought of such a kind and clever thing to do. And as for Mr. Knight, he told the story forevermore to anyone who would listen, always ending it with, "And that cat, Spider, really saved Mrs. Broom's life."

It goes without saying that Mrs. Broom and Spider are still living happily together.

Spider doesn't make faces anymore, or have tantrums, or claw people, or whine, or rush around in a frenzy. Some say it's because he's older and wiser, but others say it's because he's found someone to love.

As for Mrs. Broom, she loved Spider anyway, even when he was nasty. So she just goes on the way she always did.